My Dad Is Getting Married Again

by Lisa M. Schab, L.C.S.W.
Illustrated by Bruce Van Patter

Childswork
ChildsPLAY™
Plainview, New York

My Dad Is Getting Married Again

By Lisa M. Schab, L.C.S.W.
Illustrated by Bruce Van Patter

Childswork/Childsplay publishes products for mental health professionals, teachers and parents who wish to help children with their developmental, social and emotional growth. For questions, comments, or to request a free catalog describing hundreds of games, toys, books, and other counseling tools, call 1-800-962-1141.

© 1996 Childswork/Childsplay, LLC
A Guidance Channel Company
135 Dupont Street
Plainview, NY 11803
Tel. 1-800-962-1141

ISBN 1-882732-43-X

ACKNOWLEDGMENTS

I would like to thank my husband and friend, Bernd Harrer, for giving me the space, time, and support, to follow my talents and desires; and for sharing with me his two children, Jason and Shannon, whom I feel truly blessed to have as a part of my life.

I would also like to thank Susan Hoke, L.C.S.W., for her encouragement and guidance, and without whom this book might not have come to be.

INTRODUCTION FOR GROWN-UPS

This book was written as a tool to be used to help children and their families in dealing with the experiences of a parent's remarriage.

While school-age children would be able to read and "participate" in the story on their own, ideally at some point the book should be read with a parent and child (or helping professional and child) together, with the events and choices in the story acting as a catalyst for discussion about the child's own real experiences and feelings.

The basic message for all readers is that while remarriage takes adjustment and brings about thoughts and feelings that may be confusing or frightening, these thoughts and feelings are normal and can be worked through with time and patience.

Because change, however positive, involves the stresses of readjustment, all family members are encouraged to be gentle with themselves, with each other, and especially with children, whose sense of security and safety derives directly from their relationship with their parents.

When children, or adults, find themselves acting out their uncomfortable feelings through disruptive or inappropriate behavior, it is important to remember that this is likely a sign of the discomfort within and that love and understanding is needed just as much as limit-setting.

Readers are encouraged to give time and attention to their inner experiences of the outward change that remarriage brings. May you fare well on your journey and find joy in your new family.

INTRODUCTION FOR KIDS

When your mom and dad get divorced, there are a lot of new things to get used to.

You have to get used to your dad living in a different house from you.

You have to get used to him not being there to tuck you into bed every night.

You have to get used to talking to him on the phone a lot more, and seeing him in person a lot less.

You have to get used to doing things with only one parent at a time, because you don't usually do things all together any more.

You have to get used to telling your friends why you can't play with them on the weekends that you go to visit your dad.

You have to get used to packing your clothes and toys and homework for visits to your dad, and you have to get used to remembering to bring everything back to your mom's house again.

You have to get used to a lot of those kinds of things that happen on the outside.

And you also have to get used to the kinds of things that happen on the inside. Like that kind of sad and scary feeling that sometimes comes when you think about your mom and dad being divorced.

Sometimes, just when you think you've gotten used to things, your mom or dad throws you another new thing to get used to, on the outside and on the inside. . .

Like when your dad tells you he's going to get married again–but he's *not* going to marry your mom.

When that happens, there can be a lot of different thoughts that come into your head, and a lot of different feelings that follow them. And, there are a lot of different things that you can do with those feelings.

Some of the ways you think and act can make things easier for you, and some of the ways you think and act can make things harder.

As you read the rest of this story, you will be able to choose different thoughts to have and actions to take.

Choose whichever ones you want, and see how your choices affect the outcome. You can go back as many times as you want to and make different choices. See what happens when you do!

THE STORY BEGINS...

One day when you go to visit your dad, he says he has something very important to tell you. You wonder what it is, and you hope it's some news about getting tickets to the circus, or going on a vacation, or that your best friend can spend the night.

Instead, your dad tells you that he has decided to get married again. When he says that, you can feel your heart jump up, and a huge smile soars across your face. Yes! Your mom and dad are getting back together–just like you'd planned!

But then your dad says no, that's not quite right. He is not getting married to your mom this time. He is getting married to his girlfriend, Melanie.

The minute he says that, your smile disappears, and your heart sinks as fast as an elevator going to the very bottom floor. Your dad said he was going to marry Melanie. He's not going to marry your mom again. You had wished and hoped your hardest that your mom and dad would get back together. You had planned over and over in your head how it would happen. You had thought that if you wished hard enough, or planned it well enough, it would really happen. But it didn't work. Your biggest wish isn't going to come true.

You feel very let down. So, what do you?

If you give your dad a mean look and yell at him, "I hate you!" turn to page 6.

If you run out of the room and out the front door of the house, turn to page 9.

If you frown and hang your head down, turn to page 13.

You are feeling so bad inside that you start pounding on your dad's chest with your fists. He tries to hold your arms and tells you to calm down, but you don't want to. You are very angry, and you can feel all the angry energy coming out when you shout at your dad and hit him.

You say, "I hate you and I hate Melanie!"

Your dad gives you a pillow off of the couch and says, "Here, pound on this instead of me."

If you pound on the pillow, turn to page 7.

If you throw the pillow across the room and break a lamp, turn to page 8.

You keep pounding your fists into the couch pillow over and over again while your dad holds it for you. You can feel all your angry energy coming out through your fists, and it feels good to get rid of it! Pretty soon you start to feel more calm.

Your dad puts his arm around you and gives you a hug. "It looks like you got pretty upset when I told you I was going to marry Melanie."

You nod your head, yes.

"I'm glad you decided to get your angry feelings out on the pillow instead of me," says Dad. "Now, do you want to talk about it?"

If you say no, turn to page 17.

If you say yes, turn to page 24.

"Oh, no!" shouts your dad when he sees the lamp break. He goes over to where it has fallen and begins picking up the pieces.

"Come over here and help me," he says.

You get off the couch, but you don't move any farther. You still feel angry about him and Melanie getting married. You give your dad kind of a mean look, and he sees it.

"I can understand if you're feeling mad," Dad says. "But there are better ways to let it out. Why don't you go get a broom and use up some of that angry energy by cleaning this up? Then I think we need to have a talk."

"I'm not talking to you!" you shout. "I'm not ever talking to you again!" You run out of the room.

Turn to page 15.

8

You are feeling so upset that you want to run away. You run down the front steps and past the neighbor's house. You can hear your dad running behind you.

He calls for you to stop, but you don't want to. You are very hurt inside and you just want to get away from everybody and everything.

Your dad calls to you again, "Come on back! I want to talk to you."

If you keep running down the block, turn to page 10.

If you run into the neighbors' yard and hide behind their bushes, turn to page 11.

If you stop and let your dad catch up to you, turn to page 12.

You run as fast and as far as you can, but finally you stop because you're out of breath. You can feel your heart pounding hard. Your legs hurt. Your body is really tired. You discover that the bad feelings inside of you aren't quite as strong, but they're still there.

You hear footsteps close to you. When you look up, your dad is there.

"Come here," he says, holding out his arms.

If you walk towards him, turn to page 18.

If you turn and run the other way, turn to page 19.

Sitting in the neighbors' bushes by the sidewalk, you can see your dad walk by, calling your name. You stay as quiet as you can.

"Come on back!" calls your dad.

But you don't want to go back. You don't ever want to go back again. Not if your mom and dad aren't getting back together. Not if your dad is going to marry Melanie.

If he's going to marry Melanie, then you're never going home. When you think about it you feel all mixed up inside. You feel mad, sad, and scared. There is even one little part which feels happy, because you really like Melanie! But that only makes things more confusing. You think it would be easier just to run away.

Then you see a pair of familiar legs on the other side of the bushes. Dad has found you.

"Hi there," he says. "Do you think you're ready to come home and talk?"

If you say, "I'm never talking to you again!" turn to page 20.

If you nod your head, yes, and go home with Dad, turn to page 24.

11

Your dad comes up to you and holds out his hand. "Come on," he says. "Do you want to go home and try to work this out?"

If you say, "No! I don't want to!" turn to page 16.

If you agree and follow him back home, turn to page 24.

You are feeling so bad inside, you don't even want to look at your dad. He puts his finger under your chin and lifts your head up until you can see right into his eyes.

"What's the matter?" he asks.

You just look down again and shrug your shoulders.

"You look pretty upset," he says. "Do you want to tell me about it?"

If you say, "I think I need a hug first," turn to page 14.

If you shake your head, "No," turn to page 16.

13

"A hug?" says your dad. "Sure thing!"

He spreads out his arms and you crawl into them. It feels kind of confusing inside of you right now, but it feels safe and warm in Dad's arms. You think that even though Dad is marrying Melanie, he must still love you.

Then Dad says, "I'm glad you told me what you needed. Then I could give it to you. Now, do you want to tell me how you're feeling?"

Turn to page 24.

You run up to your room and slam the door–hard. So hard that the pictures on the wall shake. Luckily none of them fall.

You hear your dad's footsteps coming down the hall toward your room and he knocks on your door.

"Can I come in?" he asks.

"No! Go away!"

"I think you need some time to cool down," Dad says. "Unless you're ready to talk, or to clean up the broken lamp, you need to stay in your room until I call you."

If you calm down and then go find your dad, turn to page 16.

If you continue to think about how bad you feel, turn to page 23.

"Why don't you want to talk?" asks Dad.

"Because," you say, "What good is that going to do? It won't stop you from marrying Melanie. It won't get you and Mom back together again."

"Well, you're right about that," says Dad. "Usually what other people do is out of your control. But, what is in your control is what you do. You can make yourself feel better or worse depending on how you decide to handle things. Deciding to talk to me about it might make you feel better."

"Really?"

"Really."

"All right," you say. "I guess I could try."

Turn to page 24.

You feel so upset that the last thing you want to do is talk about it. You think that will only make it worse.

Plus, if you tell your dad how you feel, he might get mad at you. He might not even love you anymore.

"You don't have to be afraid to tell me your feelings," says your dad–as if he were reading your mind. "I love you, and I want to help."

"You won't get mad and hate me?" you ask.

"Absolutely not," says Dad.

"Well. . . maybe I'll talk about it."

Turn to page 24.

"You look pretty upset," your dad says.

"I guess I am," you answer.

"I think we need to talk."

"I think so, too."

Turn to page 24.

No way! you think. I'm not going with him! I'm not going back there. I'm not–I'm not–I'm not!

All of the sudden you look up and realize you don't know where you are. Nothing looks familiar. You look behind you, but you can't see your dad anymore. And you can't see his house either. You're starting to feel scared. You're starting to feel some tears well up in your eyes. Your stomach is feeling queasy.

Turn to page 21.

"Wow," says Dad. "You must be pretty upset to never want to talk to me again."

You nod your head.

"Well," he says, "I don't blame you."

"You don't?"

"No, not at all. My telling you that I'm going to marry Melanie must have brought up a lot of different feelings inside you. You have a right to those feelings."

"I do?"

"Sure you do," says Dad. "But running away or trying to hide from them won't make you feel any better.

"What will help?"

"Talking about it can help. Do you want to give it a try?"

"I guess I could."

Slowly you stand up and poke your head over the bushes. Dad lifts you the rest of the way out and you follow him home.

Turn to page 24.

"Here you are!"

Whew! It's your dad's voice.

"Come here right now," he says. "Running away won't help anything. But it could get you hurt or lost."

"But I feel awful," you say.

"I know," Dad says. "Will you give me a chance to help?"

If you say nothing, turn to page 22.

If you agree, turn to page 24.

You walk home with your dad silently the whole way. He tries to ask you some questions, but you don't want to answer. You feel like crying, but you hold the tears back. Your stomach seems like it's all tied up in knots. Your head, too.

When you get home Dad says, "You still look pretty upset."

You don't answer.

"Holding things inside will only make you feel worse," he says. "Would you rather do something that could make you feel better?"

You nod your head, yes.

Turn to page 24.

22

You think that your life is terrible. It's not fair that Dad is marrying Melanie. What about your dream for your mom and dad to get back together? Other kids you know don't have divorced parents.

It's not fair! You think again. I hate my life!

There is a box of crayons near your bed. You pick it up and take out the crayons. One by one, you start breaking them in half and throwing them against the wall.

You hear your dad's footsteps again, and he opens your door.

"I can't allow you to keep breaking things. You need to stop this right now. Are you ready to calm down and let your feelings out in a better way?"

You think about it for a minute, then finally nod, yes.

Turn to page 24.

"Okay, then why don't you tell me what's going on inside of you?"

Wow, you think. What a hard question. You're not even sure what is going on inside of you. How are you going to tell your dad? You look at him and shrug your shoulders.

Dad says, "I know this isn't easy for you. But you've done a good job of getting used to your mom and me being divorced, and I think you can get through this, too. The best way to deal with your feelings is to let them out somehow—in a way that doesn't hurt you or anybody else.

"When you express your feelings, a couple of good things happen. One is that you feel lighter inside. Another is that when you tell someone what's wrong, they might be able to help you."

He pauses. "Would you like to give it a try?"

If you say, "Okay," turn to page 25.

If you say, "I'd like to, but I don't know how to say it out loud," turn to page 26.

If you say nothing, turn to page 27.

If you say, "No!" turn to page 28.

"Good," Dad says, "Why don't you try to tell me what you're feeling inside when you think about Melanie and me getting married."

"I guess when I think about it I feel a lot of things," you say.

"That's all right," Dad says. "Start at the beginning."

Turn to page 32.

25

"Well," says your dad, "Saying it out loud isn't the only way to express your feelings. How about drawing them in a picture? Or writing them down?"

"Hey," you say, "That's a good idea! I can do that!"

If you decide to draw your feelings in a picture, turn to page 29.

If you decide to write your feelings out on paper, turn to page 30.

Y ou don't want to talk about it. Why can't Dad just leave you alone?

You walk away from him and go outside to the back yard. You crawl into the tent Dad had put up for you. You and Dad were going to sleep in it tonight, and tell ghost stories and roast marshmallows on the grill. But now you don't feel like doing any of that. And right now you have a stomach ache, so you couldn't eat marshmallows anyway.

Turn to page 31.

Why doesn't Dad understand? Why doesn't he know how awful I feel? Why doesn't he know how mad and sad and scared and confused I am?

What if Melanie tries to take my mom's place? What if after Dad marries Melanie he doesn't have enough love left for me? I've always liked Melanie, especially when she goes bike riding with me, but if she marries Dad, my wish won't come true–Mom and Dad won't ever get back together again.

You walk over to the couch and give it a hard kick.

Turn to page 34.

You and your dad find some crayons and markers and some paper to draw on. You sit down at the table and look at the big blank paper. You think about what you are feeling inside. Finally, you pick up some crayons and begin.

As you draw, you discover several different feelings inside of you. Some of them are uncomfortable, but some of them are nice. You find that as you put your feelings into pictures on the paper, you feel a lot lighter inside.

Finally you are done. You show your dad the paper.

"Wow!" he says. "You did a great job. Now tell me what these pictures are about."

Turn to page 32.

You find some notebook paper and a pencil in your backpack, and Dad lets you sit at his big desk.

At first it is hard to think of how to put your feelings into words. They seem all mixed up inside of you. You write something down, then erase it. You write something else, then scratch it out. But the next time you try, it works. And as you go along, it gets easier and easier. Before you know it, the whole page is covered with your writing. You discover that when you take your feelings from the inside of you and put them onto the paper which is outside of you, they don't seem quite as big anymore. You feel a lot lighter inside.

"Hey, Dad!" you shout. "Dad! Look what I've written."

"That's great," says Dad. "Read it to me."

Turn to page 32.

You stay in the tent for a long time, going over and over in your head how bad things are. There are so many feelings inside of you.

You are really mad, because it seems that if Melanie marries your dad, she will be taking up the space where your mom is supposed to be.

You are a little scared, too. What if after your dad marries Melanie he doesn't have any love left over for you?

You are also pretty sad. If Dad marries Melanie, that means he and your mom won't be getting back together. And that was your biggest wish in the whole world.

What makes you confused, is that deep down inside you actually *like* Melanie! She is fun and nice, and lets you lick the bowl when she bakes cookies, just like your mom.

But, you think, "She's not my mom." And you wish your stomach ache would go away. Then the tent flap opens and there is your dad.

Turn to page 34.

31

"Well, first I feel mad. Because it seems like Melanie is taking up the space where my mom is supposed to be."

"I also feel scared, because I'm afraid you might not love me as much after you're married to Melanie."

"I do feel a little happy, because I like Melanie, and when you're with her, you don't grumble and yell like you used to with Mom."

"But most of all I feel sad. Because if you marry Melanie, that means that you and Mom aren't getting back together again. And somehow, I always thought that would happen."

"Well," says your dad. "Those are quite a lot of things to feel at once. But do you know what? It's okay to have *all* those feelings at one time. And now that you've told me, maybe I can help. I want you to listen carefully, because there are some very important things I'm going to tell you."

So you climb up into Dad's lap, and he puts his arms around you and looks you straight in the eye.

"The first thing is that I love you very much, and that will not stop when I marry Melanie. I have enough love for both of you, just like you have enough love for both me and your mom.

"Second, even if Melanie is my new wife, your mom will always be your mom."

Turn to page 33

"Melanie will never take your mom's place, but she can be your friend, and be another grown-up to love and care for you."

"And third, no matter how much you may wish for it, your mom and I will never be married to each other again. That is not going to happen."

"But, even if your mom and I aren't married to each other, you are still our child and we both love you very much. That will never change."

Your dad smiles at you. "Is all of that clear?"

"Sure," you say, and breathe a little sigh of relief.

"Do you feel better now that we've talked about it?"

"Yes," you say, "I feel a lot better. I guess it's not going to be that bad."

"No," says your dad. "It's not going to be that bad at all."

THE END

"I'm sorry you're still feeling so bad, " Dad says. "I hope you decide to talk this out with me soon because I think it will make you feel better."

You don't say anything.

"I love you very much," says Dad.

"You do?" All of a sudden things seem a little less awful. "Well," you say, "Maybe by tomorrow I'll be ready to talk about it."

Dad smiles. "That's great," he says. "We'll talk tomorrow."

"Okay," you nod your head. "We'll talk tomorrow."

THE END